The Other Dog

by Madeleine L'Engle

Illustrated by Christine Davenier

chronicle books·san francisco

For my great-grandsons,
Konstantinos John Voiklis and Cooper Hindemith Roy,
who bring light to all the dark corners
—Madeleine L'Engle

For my daughter, Josephine
—Christine Davenier

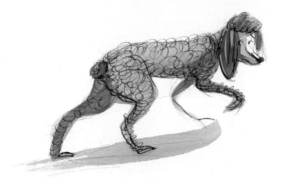

This Chronicle Books LLC hardcover edition published in 2018.
Originally published in hardcover in 2001.

Text copyright © 2001 by Crosswicks, Ltd.
Illustrations copyright © 2001 by Christine Davenier.
Illustrations in author's note are copyright © 2001 by Crosswicks, Ltd.

ISBN 978-1-4521-7189-0

The Library of Congress has cataloged the paperback edition as follows:
L'Engle, Madeleine.
The other dog / Madeleine L'Engle ; illustrated by Christine Davenier.—1st paperback ed.
p. cm.
Summary: The family poodle protests at first when the master and mistress bring home a new "dog" to share the household.
ISBN-13: 978-0-8118-5228-9 (13-digit)
ISBN-10: 0-8118-5228-8 (10-digit)
[1. Dogs—Fiction. 2. Babies—Fiction.] I. Davenier, Christine, ill. II. Title.
PZ7.L5385Ot 2006
[E]—dc22

2005018705

Manufactured in China.

Typeset in Garamond and Bookeyed Jack.

10 9 8 7 6 5 4 3 2 1

Chronicle Books LLC
680 Second Street
San Francisco, California 94107

Chronicle Books—we see things differently. Become part of our community at www.chroniclekids.com.

A few words about this book

Are you a dog person or a cat person? I've always objected to the idea that you have to be either one or the other. I, for one, have my dog moods and my cat moods, and my grandmother Madeleine did too. She had great affection for her cats, but it's also true that her dogs were the apple of her eye. She was a dog person in the same way she was a New Yorker: although she raised her children in Connecticut and loved spending time there, New York was always home.

Touché, the narrator of this story, was her first dog and first real pet. She acquired Touché while she was acting in a production of *The Cherry Orchard* on Broadway in 1944. She was living by herself for the first time, and Touché was an important consolation and comrade.

My grandmother wrote this book after she was married and had her first child, my mother, Josephine. She illustrated the manuscript herself, but couldn't find a publisher for it, and eventually put it aside. When the family moved to Northwestern Connecticut, Touché made the transition as well, and she made gracious room for the other pets that came along (including cats, which were better at catching mice). Among the beloveds were: Brillig, Chess, Sputnik, Daisy, Narcissus (Cissie), Echo, Heidi, Hans Sachs, Percy, Sheats and Kelley, Doc, Titus, Tybalt, and Tesseract.

When *The Other Dog* was finally accepted for publication about 50 years after she first wrote it, she was a great-grandmother. Tatiana, a lovely and imperious white cat, and Tino, an exuberant and affectionate Golden Retriever, were her daily companions. Her beloved Touché was long gone—but a special light came in her eyes whenever she talked about that dog. How wonderful that she got to see Touché come to life once more, in this book.

—*Charlotte Jones Voiklis*

First of all,

I think you should know that
I am the one who wrote this book.
After all (contrary to opinion),
the author of a book is very important.
Please believe me: without the author,
a book would never get written.
So, I—Touché L'Engle-Franklin—

wrote this book,
with the assistance of that
inferior canine Jo.

This summer . . .

my mistress went away for several days.
And when she came back, she brought with her
another dog.

If you ask me, this was a great waste of money.
Dogs are expensive to feed and clothe,
and one dog is enough for any family.
I fail to see why I did not satisfy all requirements.

I have beauty, wit, and charm.

I have been on the stage.

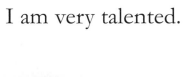

I am very talented.

And until this other dog
was brought into our home
(without warning),
my master and mistress
seemed perfectly happy with me.

I am very good about sitting on laps.
In fact, I *love* sitting on laps.
I know of no other dog
who could sit on a lap for as long as
or with as much patience as I can.

So why another dog?

I dance, oh-so-daintily,

when it is time to eat.

My master and mistress
love to look at me.

So why another dog?

I afford my master endless pleasure in his off-hours
when he bathes and clips me.
I can wear my ears long or short.
I sit still for hours while he snips off hair here and there.
No other dog would be so good and patient.

I am tremendously useful in such household tasks
as bringing home the groceries.
And I always tell my master and mistress
when the telephone or the doorbell rings.
No one could be
more efficient,
more energetic,
more conscientious,
or louder
about this than I am.

So why another dog?

But what's done is done.
The dog was brought home, and I had to learn to make the best of it.

Nevertheless, from the start I noticed
a great many mysterious and horrifying things.
For instance,
when I am taken out to get some fresh air
I always have to walk—even when it rains.
The Jo is taken out in a carriage,
and when it rains
she doesn't have to go out at all.

And another thing.
My master and mistress keep putting on
and taking off white pieces of cloth around Jo's bottom,
called, for some obscure reason, "diapers."
At first I did not understand the significance of this.
But when I did, I was deeply shocked.
When I have anything of that sort to do,
I go out into the street.
White cloths or no, I would *never* do it in the house.

At least one thing remained clear.
Of the two dogs, I was the most important.
You see, each night we would start out in our separate beds,
this dog called Jo, and I.
(Now, her bed may be a little more fancy and froufrou,
but mine is more practical.)

In the morning *she* would still be in her bed,
but *I* would not be in my bed.
Well, if that doesn't show you who's who around here,
I don't know what would.

And another thing.
This Jo-dog gets fed several times a day.
I only get fed once.
Of course, there may be a reason for this.

You see, I have frequently been told
that my tail is like a little chrysanthemum.
Jo-thing hasn't any tail at all.
Of course I am aware that, because of the dictates of fashion,
some dogs have their tails clipped.
But there is always something left.
And Jo has no tail.
Perhaps they think that if they feed her
and feed her,
she may grow a beautiful chrysanthemummy tail like mine.

And, by the way, our Jo—as well as having no tail—
has practically no hair.
Certainly not enough to brush.
So, when people come to call,
we have to put clothes on her.
All I need is a good hairbrushing.

If summer comes, can fall be far behind?
So said the poet.
Came autumn, and Jo-girl and I are almost the same size.
She has a little more hair but not much.
I am afraid she is just of an inferior breed called "baby,"
and there is nothing that can be done about it.

When the Jo-dog grew bigger
and bigger every day, and more and more rambunctious,
my master and mistress got a doghouse for her—
something I have been well-behaved enough never to need.
And now, when company comes,
I have to stay at the doghouse
and watch over our Jo.

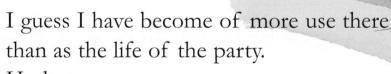

I guess I have become of more use there
than as the life of the party.
Ho hum . . .
It may be useful, but it's not nearly as much fun.
But since we have Jo-dog,
someone has to take care of her,
and I will do my part.

I must admit, though, that in our few conversations
she's been most interested in everything I've had to say—

which is, I think, a definitely encouraging
sign of intelligence.

Therefore, I must admit that
in spite of myself . . .
in spite of the Jo-girl . . .
in spite of everything . . .
I am getting very fond of our other dog.
So, somehow or other, I have come to the
unpredictable,
surprising,
amazing,
astonishing,
astounding conclusion:

in every home there should be
at least two dogs!

So now good-bye—and lots of love.

Touché

Author's Note

Touché, a little grey poodle, came into my life when she was bought—for an exorbitant sum, I thought—during the rehearsals for Eva Le Gallienne's production of Chekhov's *The Cherry Orchard*. Of course, all the actors with dogs had wanted their pets in the show, but these other dogs were either intimidated by being in the theatre or, if they passed that first test, were undone by the noise of the party scene. So in came Touché, a born actress who wasn't in the least intimidated by the laughter and song of the party scene; she was quickly hired. Someone had to take care of her before and after the show, and I (the general understudy, who did everything that wasn't specified in the script) was lucky enough to get the job.

By the time the show was over, Touché and I had definitely "bonded," and there was no taking her away from me. By that time, Touché was thoroughly addicted to the adulation she received on stage. "Oh, that marvelous little dog! How did you teach her? She trains so easily! Can't you give her a little more to do? The audience adores her in that scene when she jumps up and tries to comfort—"

At this point Eva Le Gallienne would protest, a little wistfully, "That's supposed to be my scene." I could understand Le Gallienne's point of view.

There were a few less easily solved problems. For instance, travel. I lived in Greenwich Village. The theatre was in midtown. There was no way I could afford, on my Equity minimum salary, to take Touché back and forth in a taxi. So what to do?

I thought it over, and then I slung her over my shoulders like a feather boa, and she obediently hung there until we got to the stage door alley. Wherever I went, Touché went with me.

When Hugh Franklin was cast as Petya Trofimov, the young student who is Chekhov's mouthpiece, I expected the usual jealous annoyance from Touché. Not at all. Touché gave Hugh an appraising look, an interested sniff, and decided that he was all right. To my surprise, she let him brush her. She chose him to be her groom.

She did not come to our tiny little wedding, but otherwise she was with us night and day. And every evening, at the close of the play, she had her own special curtain call. We had to cut her down to one curtain

call only, because she danced around and waved her paws at the audience and tended to take over the show, and the other actors complained.

When we had our first baby, I sat on the sofa nursing her, and Touché sat beside me, nursing a pink rubber hippopotamus. When she had her first litter, she was less concerned about the puppies than she was about her hippopotamus. She did her duty, but she wasn't really interested. But Touché and the puppies were so charming together that I took colored pencils and began sketching them. And that was the beginning of this book.

Her first love remained her true love: the theatre. There are not a great many roles written for a small grey poodle, but she did play Flush, Elizabeth Barrett's spaniel, in *The Barretts of Wimpole Street*. There's no way Touché looked like a spaniel; we just counted on her acting ability. The show had a long run, and Touché was happy. After it closed, everybody wanted to take Touché home—but she was mine, there was no questioning that.

There were no more plays at that time with dogs in the cast. But she had the best of everything that I could

give her—a warm green wool coat in cold weather, and little boots for mud. She hated the boots, so I stopped fighting her about them. *I* might not want to go barefooted in winter weather, but then, I don't have fur between my toes.

She ate well: we gave her ground beef, not the prepared ground beef, full of fat, but specially ground top round. If she was "off her feed," I fed her by hand. Unlike most dogs, her theatre training had taught her to like the spotlight—even for her private functions, she sought a streetlamp before she squatted to pee. And we were expected to have tissues ready to wipe her for bigger business. And when she had accomplished everything, she expected applause.

She lived with us happily until her kidneys failed, and she died quietly one night, lying between us on our bed. An era was ended, and things would never be the same.

—Madeleine L'Engle